Skeleton Valley

PRAISE FOR *STORYSHARES*

"One of the brightest innovators and game-changers in the education industry."
– Forbes

"Your success in applying research-validated practices to promote literacy serves as a valuable model for other organizations seeking to create evidence-based literacy programs."
- Library of Congress

"We need powerful social and educational innovation, and Storyshares is breaking new ground. The organization addresses critical problems facing our students and teachers. I am excited about the strategies it brings to the collective work of making sure every student has an equal chance in life."
– Teach For America

"Around the world, this is one of the up-and-coming trailblazers changing the landscape of literacy and education."
- International Literacy Association

"It's the perfect idea. There's really nothing like this. I mean wow, this will be a wonderful experience for young people."   - Andrea Davis Pinkney, Executive Director, Scholastic

"Reading for meaning opens opportunities for a lifetime of learning. Providing emerging readers with engaging texts that are designed to offer both challenges and support for each individual will improve their lives for years to come. Storyshares is a wonderful start."
- David Rose, Co-founder of CAST & UDL

Skeleton Valley

Tom Rameaka

STORYSHARES

Story Share, Inc.
New York. Boston. Philadelphia

Published in the United States by Story Share, Inc.

The characters and events in this book are fictitious. Any similarity to real persons, living or dead, is entirely coincidental.

Storyshares
Story Share, Inc.
24 N. Bryn Mawr Avenue #340
Bryn Mawr, PA 19010-3304
www.storyshares.org

Inspiring reading with a new kind of book.

Interest Level: Middle School
Grade Level Equivalent: 3.7

9781642611823

Book design by Storyshares

Printed in the United States of America

Storyshares Presents

1

It was the last day of summer vacation. I woke with the strange feeling that *it was gonna happen today.*

The morning began much earlier than I wanted it to. I planned on sleeping until noon, just because I could. That would be taken away when school started in the fall. I would have to catch the bus at the end of the street by 6:45.

All that boring summer of 1968, I kept waiting for something *different* to happen. Nothing exciting occurred in Cranston, Rhode Island.

I had turned fourteen in April and felt that I was finally shedding the stigma of being unlucky number thirteen. I mean, everybody makes a big deal out of becoming a teenager. What they don't mention is that thirteen is the lowest form of it.

Besides being a popularly unlucky number, you don't just suddenly become a card-carrying member of the teen world. Somehow, I'd expected to be able to do more than I had before. I mean, "teen" would now be hooked onto the end of my age for the next six years! Freedom, right? Not a chance.

Getting a driver's license was a long three years away. My parents still gave me the same old nine o'clock curfew. Most of the older kids still ignored me. It's not like the zits on my face were some terminal disease.

Even worse, I didn't even grow much taller. Only one girl in my class spoke to me like I wasn't gum on the bottom of her shoe. Beautiful Janice Rodriguez still had me by at least two inches. I was definitely in love with her, but how can you ever ask a girl who looks down on the top of your head to dance?

Anyway, turning fourteen and going into the eighth grade was going to be different. My face was clearing up. I had actually grown an inch or so. Hopefully, I thought,

Janice's growth spurt was over. School started Monday, so I wouldn't know until then.

Meanwhile, I scarfed down my second bowl of Wheaties, the Breakfast of Champions™, and thought about what to do on my last day of vacation.

2

I decided to call my best friend Leon. I was going to talk him into finally hiking up to Skeleton Valley. We talked about doing this when school let out last June.

But every time I called him, Leon had another excuse. I knew he was mowing several neighbors' lawns. He also babysat his little sister while his mom worked.

But there was something else. Leon had changed. I still couldn't figure out why. This was the first summer that we hadn't hung out together.

Leon and I had been friends since kindergarten. We connected the very first day of school, probably because neither of us could sit still for more than five minutes. We loved the sand table. Our teacher Mrs. Baker, gave us a free pass whenever our squirming became distracting. We'd been, like my mom said, "Two peas in a pod," ever since. Except this summer.

I guess I should point out that Leon's Black, and I'm White. Not that it should matter, but back in 1968, it was not very common to see a friendship like ours. Neither of us ever noticed this, though. We were too busy pushing toy bulldozers through the sand back in kindergarten. It wasn't until, I guess, the third grade that this difference was brought to my attention.

I was headed outside to meet Leon at our fort in the woods. I had just snuck a half loaf of Wonder Bread and a jar of peanut butter into my knapsack. Then, I heard my mom's voice coming from the hallway. I knew she was talking to her friend Judy. Her voice always dropped to a whisper and then was followed by a mass of giggles.

As I stepped through the screen door, I heard her say something that made me stop. "No," she said, "I can talk longer. Timmy's headed out to play with his little colored friend Leon."

I was so shocked. I almost let the door hit me in the head. Little *colored* friend? I was truly confused. Leon was colored? Like crayons? Was I also colored? Did Leon's mom tell her friends that he played with a colored boy? I thought about this on my way to meet him. Exactly what color was he?

I remembered my big box of crayons that had the built-in sharpener. Leon was a bit like the color brown. Then again, I thought, he wasn't really. Maybe more a mixture of burnt umber and brown. Then, I had it. He was like the same color as YooHoo, my favorite drink. Kind of a warm, caramel color. Then, I stopped and looked at my arm. What color was I? Kind of a reddish tan.

I don't remember ever mentioning my mom's words to Leon. Like most eight year olds, we were more focused on having fun. All we knew was we both loved playing in our forts together. We would spend hours building them. We'd then tear them down and start over. We had the most fun defending them against terrifying armies. Of course, they only existed in our imaginations.

I thought again how different this summer had been from the others. My friendship with Leon wasn't the same.

I think it all started in April. My family had just finished dinner. My dad, as usual, turned on the TV to watch Walter

Cronkite. He never missed watching Walter give the nightly news. I was heading out to the garage with a big bag of garbage.

I stopped when I heard the famous newsman's voice grow somber.

"On this day, April fourth, at six o'clock Eastern Standard Time, Dr. Martin Luther King was shot dead. The most famous Negro in America was standing on the balcony of his motel."

I remember dropping the bag of garbage on the floor and hearing my mom cry out, "That's just horrible! What is happening to this world!"

I quickly scooped up the trash. I went outside and put it in the metal garbage can next to our garage.

I thought of my friend Leon.

He had written a report on Martin Luther King that year. He looked so proud when it was his turn to read it to the class. I remember Leon looking up at everyone at the end of his report. He had this big grin on his face.

He told us that Dr. King just won the Nobel Peace Prize. He explained to us that this great man preached nonviolence. Dr. King did this even though Black people were treated badly in many places.

I felt proud, too, knowing that I went to school in a place where everyone was treated the same. Leon was one of only half a dozen Black kids in our school. In my thirteen years of experience, I hadn't seen anyone treat him differently. I don't think I ever did . . . or maybe I wasn't paying very good attention.

He was just Leon, my best friend.

Remembering this, I decided right then to hop on my bike and go to Leon's house. I yelled to my parents that I'd be right back, and took off.

Skeleton Valley

3

Leon only lived about a mile away. It was a short ride across the small river from where we lived. I never noticed how much smaller Leon's house was than mine until that day.

I rode up his street and saw about five cars in front of his one-story, ranch-style home. There must have been twenty people gathered around his front door.

My first thought was, no way can all those people fit in that house! I knew because I'd been in it many times. His mom always greeted me with a smile and a hug.

Leon's little sister, Mary Beth, always wanted to hang out with us. We allowed her to for a short time. Then we always headed outside to our secret fort.

I got off my bike, leaned it against a tree, and looked around for Leon. I spotted his mom talking to a few people by the front steps. She gave me a small wave and turned back into the house.

A few of the people by the front door looked my way. They seemed to scowl at me. Huh?

"Everybody's pretty broken up about Dr. King," a soft voice said behind me. Mary Beth had somehow quietly come up behind me, as she usually did. She was no longer the little kid who used to bug us so much. Even though she was two years younger, she was almost as tall as me.

She always greeted me with a laugh and a "hey Shorty!" It was our private joke because I always called her "Shrimp."

Only this time, there was no twinkle in her big brown eyes. I saw only sadness. She looked like she had just gotten over a good cry.

"I heard," I said. "Where's Leon?"

"He's in his room. Been there since Aunt Jessie called with the news. Best not to bother him." Then Mary Beth looked at me. She whispered, "In fact, no offense, Timmy, but I don't think you should come around here for awhile."

She saw the shocked look on my face. "It's not anything you did wrong, Timmy. It's . . . it's just that you're a . . . White person."

"What!"

Mary Beth said one more thing to me before she walked away. "A White person killed Dr. King."

I don't even remember getting back on my bike and riding home. I knew how much Leon loved Dr. King. He must have practiced his oral report on me ten times. I mean, I could have given the report. I recalled all his hard work doing research.

Martin Luther King was a minister. He led the 1955 Bus Boycott in Montgomery, Alabama. Black people refused to ride the city buses. They did this until they were allowed to sit anywhere they wanted. This was an example of a non-violent protest.

I remember being amazed that Martin Luther King was really smart. He even skipped the ninth and twelfth grades. He went to college, even though he really didn't graduate from high school.

I knew I wasn't that smart. Leon and I laughed about how funny it would be if he and his friend Shorty showed up at college at age sixteen.

"Yeah," he said."Can you see us dancing with all those pretty college girls?"

I also remembered this one line that Leon quoted. It was from Dr. King's "I Have a Dream" speech. It was something about how he dreamed that his four little children would not be judged by the color of their skin. He felt they should be judged by what kind of people they were.

I remember, then, feeling strange. I felt like there were so many things I didn't know about the real world.

I watched the news.

There were riots in a lot of the big cities. Black people were angry. It was horrifying seeing the police beating Black people and knocking them off their feet with fire hoses. For what? I guess I was too young to understand it all.

My parents would just shake their heads. They'd remind me how lucky I was to live in such a peaceful town.

Sometimes, I wished that Leon and I could just sit in our little fort in the woods forever. We found safety behind the old stick and plywood walls.

Now, with the death of Martin Luther King, our sheltered little world had changed. Leon didn't come to school for a few days that spring. The teachers in school avoided talking about the murder.

4

There was a change in our class that spring. It was if our innocent joy was stolen from us. Leon wasn't the same after that. We never really talked about Dr. King. Maybe that was a mistake. If we could ignore it, maybe it would go away. Maybe things could go back to the way they were. That didn't work.

Leon refused to play in the fort anymore. I have to admit, by the end of seventh grade, I felt a bit foolish thinking of playing there, too. We still shot hoops, played catch, and sat together on the bus. But something had gone out of our friendship. The easy way we used to talk to and tease each other was gone. In its place was something forced.

Some days, we played and didn't speak more than ten words to each other. I tried to explain it to my dad. He listened but said something about us growing up, how things change between people. His words didn't help me understand things any better.

On this last day of summer vacation, I decided on one more attempt to get my old friend back. I was shocked when he actually answered the phone.

"Hey, Shorty."

"Hey back. Did you know this is the last day of summer vacation? This is it, man. Eighth grade, then onto high school. We gotta do something today, Leon. Remember how we talked about hiking up to Skeleton Valley and looking for arrowheads? Let's do it! I'll get my mom to pack us a lunch. I'll even ask her to cut the crusts off your PB and J sandwich like you love. Come on, this might be our last chance! Once school begins, with homework and basketball practice, we'll never find the time."

I finally took a breath. I tried to speak quickly to make my case. I didn't want Leon to make another excuse not to hang out.

There was a moment's hesitation on the other end of the line. *Uh oh, here it comes.*

Then Leon surprised me. He said, "Okay. You're right. Why not? I'll see you in thirty."

* * *

As we headed up Reservoir Avenue, the day couldn't have been more beautiful. It was like the warm sun, bright green trees, and choruses of birds had a big meeting. At this gathering, they announced, "Let's give all the school kids one last summer vacation day to remember. When they are sitting in their stuffy, little classrooms, they'll have something to look out the window and remember. Maybe that'll keep them going until next summer."

Even Leon seemed to finally perk up. I waited for him out in my yard. I could see him cross the bridge over the river. I had watched him cross that river a thousand times. When he got to the middle, he always stopped and looked around for a stone. He then threw it, side-armed, as hard as he could. When he arrived at my house, I knew if he had a smirk on his face that he had set a new personal record for skips.

This time, he didn't stop and throw a stone. There were definitely no smiles.

He walked like he carried a backpack full of stones. Instead of flopping down on the grass next to me, he just stood on the sidewalk in front of my house.

"You all set?" he asked.

I pushed myself up and grabbed the brown sack with four sandwiches (two without the crust), two apples, and two cans of Coca-Cola. We didn't talk much on the way to Skeleton Valley. Any attempt at small talk was met with a grunt from him.

"Think the Celtics will win another championship?"

"Maybe."

"Guess the Red Sox are out of it."

"Guess so."

If those two topics didn't get Leon talking, nothing would. We walked on in silence. The only sound heard was the slap of our Converse Chuck Taylor All Stars on the street.

I wore white low tops. Leon favored the black high tops of his favorite team. He loved Bill Russell, the Celtics center and probably the best player in the NBA. Back in 1968, Russell was an outspoken Black man. It was something rarely seen in sports, let alone in Boston. Leon told me he admired Bill Russell because he never took any guff, on or off the court.

I tried another topic.

"Hey Leon, you remember when I had to stay in for detention? It was that last week of school?"

Leon let loose a small smile. "Yeah, for swinging on the stage curtain during recess."

"Man that was fun. My butt was sore for a week from landing in the first row of seats." We both laughed. I could feel the old Leon slowly coming around again. "Anyway, while I was in the library doing my time, I came across this old book. The title was *Ghost Stories of Old Rhode Island*. Every day that week, I read a different story. Some were lame, but some were pretty scary. There was one story that made my hair stand on end. It was called, 'Skeleton Valley'."

Leon stopped. He almost left skid marks on the pavement. *Ah-hah*, I thought, *now I have your attention*.

"Huh?"

"Yeah, Skeleton Valley, the place we're headed to right now."

"Nah, it must of been some other place with the same name. This place ain't famous enough to be in a story," Leon said. We began walking again.

"Ahem, remember the name of the book where I found this story?"

"Oh right," he said, "Something about ghost stories of Rhode Island."

"Of 'Old' Rhode Island. Didn't you ever wonder why this place has the horrible name of Skeleton Valley?"

"Not really, but I bet you're going to tell me."

5

Finally, I had my best friend's attention. I wanted to ask him where he'd been all summer. I wanted to tell him how awful I felt about the death of Martin Luther King.

I *needed* to tell him that I thought I knew how he felt. Robert F. Kennedy, the brother of President John F. Kennedy, was murdered just two months after Dr. King.

I knew, like Leon and me, that RFK and Dr. King were good friends. They believed in the same things, like treating each other with respect. Now they were both gone. It seemed unbelievable. Maybe the whole country was going down the tubes.

Of course, I didn't stop to think that the story of Skeleton Valley was just that: a story about death. Looking back, I think we both had that topic on our minds. Telling a ghost story was maybe safer than talking about the real thing.

We continued our hike towards Skeleton Valley. It was only about two miles from my house. I tried to remember the details from the book. I had read it only a few months before. I talked and talked until we finally entered the main trail. It led up to the top of the long, rocky climb. Finally, the trail ended, looking down upon Skeleton Valley. About halfway up, we stopped under a huge, old red oak tree. It had to be over two hundred years old. Its trunk could have been circled by about ten kids our size.

It was the only place we knew we'd get enough shade to eat lunch.

"Okay, so let's see if I got this right," said Leon between bites of PB and J. You're saying this whole area, including our neighborhoods, used to be a Narragansett Indian village?"

"Mhmm," I nodded my head up and down while wiping jelly off my chin. Washing a bite of my sandwich down with a swig of coke, I continued. "Cranston, Rhode Island, was purchased from the American Indians in 1638 by Roger Williams." We both knew about Roger Williams from history class. Plus, there was a park named after him not far from our school.

"Anyway, this town used to be called Pawtuxet. The Narragansett Indians lived here long before the White people settled this area. The Narragansetts were made up of several sub-tribes. Each tribe had its own chief. In the story, they called him the tribe's Sachem."

"Yeah, I remember that unit we did on American Indians in social studies," Leon said. "Until the *White men* came, they were a peaceful people. They survived by farming corn, hunting, and fishing."

I noticed that Leon put a special push on the words "White men."

I knew this had to do with Martin Luther King's murder. I knew it was pointless to get into an argument. I felt like my best friend was slowly coming around. I just nodded and continued. "Well, the American Indians weren't always peaceful with each other, either. They hated a tribe called the Pequots who lived mostly in Massachusetts and Connecticut.

In fact, they joined the White Puritans in a war against the Pequots."

Leon took a last bite of his apple and threw it off the trail into some high weeds. "So what does all this have to do with Skeleton Valley?"

"That's what I'm getting to," I said. "So, the Sachem of the tribe around here was called Metacom, but the English called him King Phillip for some reason. He and the other chiefs got really angry at the White people for taking over so much land. It was land that they had lived on way before the Europeans came here. It got so bad that another war started. This time it was a war between the Narragansett tribe and the White settlers. They called it 'King Phillip's War.'"

Leon stood up then. "Huh, as if *he* started the whole thing!" He picked up a stone and whipped it at a tree across the way. I could always tell when he was upset.

"The war ended in 1637, after Metacom was captured. They cut off his head! Some members of his tribe escaped to Canada. Others were shipped off as slaves to the West Indies."

Leon looked at me like I just stole his lunch money. "Man, that is the worst story I ever heard."

"Sorry," I said. "I thought since we're hiking up here it would be kind of cool . . ."

"Cool? To do what? Eat lunch in a place that was stolen from the people who lived here their whole lives?"

"Uh, no. The story went on to tell about how the ghost of Metacom still searches these hills and valleys for his head."

"WHAT!"

"I thought we could, like, help him find it."

Leon looked at me like I'd suddenly lost *my* head. He picked up his coke and took one last gulp. He shot it like a basketball into my open pack next to the tree.

I held my breath. He continued to stare at me. I was sure he was going to walk back home. Then, he surprised me.

"Okay, what are we waiting for? Any ideas where we start?"

I tried to keep the big grin off my face. "Matter of fact, I think I do."

The book, *Ghost Stories of Old Rhode Island*, had left me some clues.

6

I talked as we continued up the trail.

"The story, 'Skeleton Valley', spoke a lot about the old Sachem, Metacom. It seemed a headless ghost had been spotted a few times. A group of Boy Scouts had a campsite in Skeleton Valley in late August of the 1950s.

"One scout witnessed a mysterious light. He had gotten up to pee. As he headed back to his tent, something had caught his eye. He later claimed that he'd seen a misty human shape wandering around some big rocks. At one point, the ghostly figure looked like it was digging. According to the Scout, it had no head!"

"Man, that is weird!" said Leon.

"I figured we 'd look for those rocks. We may have a chance of finding Metacom's skull."

Leon looked around. "Uh, there's a ton of rocks around here, Timmy. How on earth can we find the ones that Metacom was digging around?"

I smiled as if I just played a great game of poker. "Because the Scout said that one of the rocks looked just like a skull!"

"No way!"

We stuffed the wrappers from lunch in my pack. Heading back up the trail, we kept looking for skull-shaped rocks. It was hard hiking as the sun blazed down on us. A few times, one of us noticed a rock that looked much like a skull. By the time we got closer, it ended up looking not quite not right.

"This is a wild goose chase," said Leon. Like me, he wiped the sweat from his face with his shirt. Even I began to wonder if the whole story was made up. Some joker trying to spook people.

I sat down on a big rock by the side of the trail. "Just a few more hundred feet, and we'll be at the top. Then, we can scan the whole valley from there," I said.

I was hot and tired. I guess too much laying around this summer had caught up with me. With effort, I pushed myself up off the rock.

We began the final trudge to the top of Skeleton Valley.

Leon and I noticed something different right away. Up ahead through some skinny trees, our eyes took in a weird sight. There were objects hanging like giant butterfly pupas, about two feet off the ground between four long stakes. We looked at each other, baffled, and crept forward, staying close to the ground.

When we were about six feet away, the hanging objects became more clear to us.

7

"Sleeping bags?" We both whispered together. *What were six sleeping bags doing hanging from poles up on this ridge above Skeleton Valley?*

I cupped my hand around Leon's ear. "Do you think anyone's sleeping in them?"

"Uh, I don't think I want to find out. We gotta get out of here!" Leon began to turn around, but I caught his elbow. "What?" he hissed.

"Look." I pointed to the bags. They were made out of a dark green canvas. You could see a big zipper all the way around one side. They looked like they could fit a person my dad's size. "What do you see?"

Leon looked at me as if I had lost all my marbles. "Uh, I see a bunch of sleeping bags, dummy."

I ignored this and said, "Yeah, but they're all kind of squishy and they haven't moved at all."

Leon stared again at the bags. "Huh. Okay, so they're empty. Nobody's in them. Why would anybody be sleeping this late in the morning anyway? It's almost noon."

"Exactly. Let's get closer so we can look down into the valley. Whoever owns these must be off hiking or something. Maybe they're looking for Metacom's skull, too!"

"What if someone down below sees us? Where are we going to hide? Those posts are too skinny . . . We'll be spotted for sure."

I smiled. I had an idea. "Listen, Leon, if we crawl real low in that high grass, we can reach the bags. Then, all we have to do is unzip them and crawl inside. We can scope out the whole valley from inside the bag. No one will see us!"

Again, Leon gave me that look. "Are you crazy?"

Then, I pulled out the ace in my deck that always worked with him. "What, are you chicken or something?"

This time, I got a very different look from my friend. This look said, *Back off!*

Leon was the bravest guy I knew, but his one weakness was that he never turned down a dare. One time, he jumped off a forty foot high train trestle into a river. We'd all heard stories about there being nasty things in that river. Old washers and rusty cars. All it took was someone saying, "I dare you," and the next thing we saw was Leon's body falling through the air.

Now, as I look back, I think I know why he did this. Leon was the only Black kid in our class. I think he felt he had to prove himself smarter and braver than all us White kids. Back then, none of us picked up on this.

Now, well, I guess I can understand it.

He took a look over his shoulder, back down the trail. Then he looked at the sleeping bags. I knew I had him then. Without a word, he began a slow crawl to the hanging bags.

We both got to the first bag at the same time. We propped ourselves up on our elbows. Staring at the valley below, we both gasped. We had expected to see the greenfields of Skeleton Valley. I remembered a small creek running through the center. A few weeping willows lined its edges.

We both must have had our mouths open for about two minutes. Finally, I found my voice. "Uh, Leon, what's the U.S. Army doing camped out in Skeleton Valley?"

Below us, we saw about twenty large green tents. They were each about the size of my family's two-car garage. A bunch of army vehicles were scattered about. We saw about seven or eight big trucks, the ones with the canvas coverings on the back. There were also a few small jeeps parked next to each tent.

"Awesome," I whispered, turning to Leon. He started to crawl away from the sleeping bags, but I caught his ankle and held on tight.

Leon looked back at me with a face I'd never seen him wear before. *Fear.* This wasn't like him. He was never scared.

Not even in sixth grade, when we'd both been sent down to the principal's office. We'd gotten punished for laughing when Carol Burns vomited in class.

Holding Leon's ankle, I pulled him back to me. He was moving his arms and kicking his legs. It was like he thought he could swim back to the trail and off the ridge. I almost lost it. He looked so comical.

"What's *wrong* with you?" I whispered.

"Nothin!"

I finally dragged him back to me. I saw tears in his eyes. *Wow!* Leon never cried either. Something definitely was wrong. He finally stopped struggling. He either was too tired to continue, or he'd just given up. He looked at me. Then, he pointed his finger at the army camp below.

"Don't you get it?" he said softly. "That's the Army National Guard down there."

I looked back down into the valley. I could see a bunch of soldiers moving around. One guy looked like he was digging something out of the ground. *Could they be looking for Metacom's skull, too?*

"Cool," I said, "It's the National Guard. So what?"

Leon looked at me again. I almost couldn't meet his eyes. They looked so angry and sad at the same time. "So what? So *what*!? Don't you ever watch the news? Those are the guys that have been beating up on Black people. Ever since Dr. King was killed, all you see is these soldiers in the streets. You see them pushing and shoving people around. If they see my Black face, they'll do the same to me! Don't you get it? They hate Black people!"

I just stared at him, then looked back down the valley. I had seen soldiers in city streets on the news, but I never thought that they might be causing harm to people. Then again, in 1968, soldiers were not treated like heroes. The Vietnam War was very unpopular. People all over the country hated it. I saw the protesters on TV. Even some soldiers coming back from the war protested. People on TV screamed at the men who'd fought.

It was confusing. Leon and I loved playing soldiers in our fort. We thought guys in the army were the best.

Now, looking at Leon's scared face, I didn't know what to think anymore.

8

The sound of pounding feet tore my mind from these thoughts.

While we were lying in the grass upon that ridge, the U.S. Army was busy. I remember thinking we were so cool, spying on the National Guard like we were. *But the joke was on us*! They'd spotted us the moment we crawled to the sleeping bags. I felt like a scared, stupid little kid when six big pairs of black boots appeared in a circle around us.

We had our heads down on our arms. I hoped I wouldn't wet my pants. We could hear the harsh breaths of the men standing above us. I peeked up and saw a face scowling down at mine. I felt frozen with fear.

"Get up, kids!" said a deep, loud voice. "NOW!"

We scrambled to our feet. I was so scared I couldn't look at the soldiers around us. *Were they going to beat us? Slap us around? Put us in shackles?* I glanced at Leon. After what he'd told me, I knew he had to be even more scared than me.

Wrong. He was smiling! *What the . . .?*

One soldier had his hand on Leon's shoulder. It was a Black hand. My eyes followed it up the arm. It was attached to the body of a smiling soldier. Two other Black soldiers were right beside him.

"What's going on, little man?" the smiling one said, looking down at Leon.

"Nothin' much," said Leon. For some reason, this got everyone laughing. *Nothing much!* Just another boring day getting captured by the National Guard! By now, they were all laughing. My heart started slowing down. I looked at Leon. He pointed to the soldier in front of me.

"This is my cousin Bethany's boyfriend, Carl. Carl, this is my best friend, Timmy. I didn't know you were in the Army."

Best. Friend. Those two words made me feel better than I had all summer. I stuck out my hand. "Glad to meet you, sir." I threw in the sir mostly because it seemed the right thing to do with a soldier.

The hand that gripped mine was huge. I was ready to have my hand crushed. Instead, a light, quick shake was all that came.

"Sorry to put such a fright in you guys," Carl said. "You didn't know it, but you were in danger." He pointed to some woods to our right. "Through those trees is our target range. We were just about to start up when someone radioed us from below. They spotted you when you left the trail and headed for the sleeping bags. We didn't want you to wander toward the range. You might get injured, or worse. So, we turned you two guys into a little field exercise. How'd we do?"

"We didn't see you coming until you were right on top of us," said Leon.

The soldiers puffed out their chests a bit.

"The Army National Guard has one mission. Serve and protect," said Carl.

I could almost hear Leon's mind going to work, then.

9

Maybe the things you see on TV aren't always the whole story. I looked around at the soldiers standing before us.

Take those uniforms off them, and they were just ordinary guys. They each had families. Some of them probably even loved the Red Sox as much as Leon and me. They probably got scared, and even did stupid things. They were . . . *human.* Just like us.

I guess Leon had a different picture of soldiers than I did. My image was of cool, brave, fighting men. His was of angry, Black-hating, White soldiers. We both had to rethink this.

"What do you say we get you guys off this ridge?" asked Carl. "How would you like a tour of the camp? We only set up once a month. You just happened to pick the wrong day to stumble upon our camp."

"Or, maybe the right day!" said Leon.

Everybody laughed again as we marched with the six soldiers down to the camp.

We had the best last day of summer vacation ever. I got to tell the story of Chief Metacom and his missing skull. I told it as we all ate some hot dogs. An officer said he'd have the men keep an eye out for any skull-shaped rocks. He even took my phone number. And it was one soldier's birthday, so cake and ice cream topped off our day.

At one point I looked over at Leon. It was good to see him laughing with his cousin's boyfriend.

Carl and another soldier drove us back to Leon's house in an Army jeep. It was the best ride we ever took.

* * *

Two days later, Leon and I sat in English class. Mrs. McGee had given us our first big writing assignment. On the black board, written in big, white letters was: *What did you do this summer?*

I looked over at Leon.

He was already writing.

About The Author

Tom Rameaka, a retired teacher from Connecticut, remembers being a boy during the turbulence of the Civil Rights, which is reflected in the first book he wrote for the Storyshares library, *Skeleton Valley*.

Skeleton Valley

About The Publisher

Story Shares is a nonprofit focused on supporting the millions of teens and adults who struggle with reading by creating a new shelf in the library specifically for them. The ever-growing collection features content that is compelling and culturally relevant for teens and adults, yet still readable at a range of lower reading levels.

Story Shares generates content by engaging deeply with writers, bringing together a community to create this new kind of book. With more intriguing and approachable stories to choose from, the teens and adults who have fallen behind are improving their skills and beginning to discover the joy of reading. For more information, visit storyshares.org.

Easy to Read. Hard to Put Down.

Skeleton Valley